W9-BTC-535

# LiAR,
# LiaR

## ALSO BY GARY PAULSEN

# GARY PAULSEN

# LIAR, LIAR

## The Theory, Practice and Destructive Properties of Deception

WENDY
LAMB
BOOKS

Text copyright © 2011 by Gary Paulsen
Jacket art copyright © 2011 by James Bernardin

Visit us on the Web! www.randomhouse.com/kids
Educators and librarians, for a variety of teaching tools, visit us at
www.randomhouse.com/teachers

*Library of Congress Cataloging-in-Publication Data*
Paulsen, Gary.
    Liar, liar : the theory, practice, and destructive properties of deception / Gary Paulsen. — 1st ed.
        p. cm.
    Summary: Fourteen-year-old Kevin is very good at lying and finds that doing so makes life easier, but when he finds himself in big trouble with his friends, family, and teachers, he must find a way to end his lies forever.
    ISBN 978-0-385-74001-2 (trade) — ISBN 978-0-385-90817-7 (lib. bdg.)
    ISBN 978-0-375-89868-6 (ebook) — ISBN 978-0-375-86611-1 (pbk.)
    [1. Honesty—Fiction. 2. Interpersonal relations—Fiction. 3. Middle schools—Fiction. 4. Schools—Fiction. 5. Family problems—Fiction. 6. Humorous stories.]
    I. Title. II. Title: Theory, practice, and destructive properties of deception.
    PZ7.P2843Li 2011
    [Fic]—dc22
                2010028356

Printed in the United States of America
10 9 8 7 6 5 4
First Edition

*This book is dedicated*
*with gratitude and respect*
*to Barbara Perris,*
*my longtime copy editor,*
*fiercely protective of my writing,*
*the elements of style and grammar,*
*and getting the details right.*

# FOREWORD

I'm the best liar you'll ever meet.

I should be good; I've had a lot of practice. I'm only fourteen, but I've known for as long as I can remember that there will be times when I'm going to have to tell a lie. It's a universal rule, a cosmic inevitability.

If you ask me, people who say honesty is the best policy are just terrible liars.

I'm good because I make it easy for people to believe me.

See, people only listen for what they want to hear, so I only tell them that.

I tell my parents what they expect—school went

well and I had a good day; yes, I did my homework; dinner was great; I'd love to drive 116 miles to go to a flea market and look for antique cookie jars and old political memorabilia with you and Dad this weekend; and no, I don't have any dirty dishes under my bed.

I tell my friends versions of what they've already said to me—yeah, the new girl is hot; Coach is psychotic to have us run suicides in gym; I'm not gonna read the whole book either; the Cubs don't have decent relief pitching but will probably clinch the division this year anyway.

I tell my teachers what they want me to say—yes, I understand the equation and how you solve it; I missed the foreshadowing until you pointed it out, but now it's as clear as day; I really do have to use the bathroom and I don't just want to walk around the halls during class wasting my time; no, I didn't see who lobbed that apple across the cafeteria, nearly taking out the lunch lady's eye (by the way, that apple missed her by a mile; everyone knows Neil Walker throws like a girl).

If you look at it from the right point of view, lying is just good manners.

Lying is my second language, a habit, a way of life.

It's gotten so that it's easier for me to lie than to tell the truth, because lying is all about common sense. Not to mention self-preservation.

I don't think I'm good enough to beat a lie detector test, but most of the time I've pretty much got everyone I know right where I want them.

Lying makes my life and—let's face it—everyone else's, too, so much better. So really, I lie for the greater good. I've come to believe that it's almost my duty. Like I'm some kind of superhero who uses his power for society. I like to think I'm doing my bit to make the world a better place—one lie at a time.

I'm not bragging or being conceited. I'm just making what they call objective observations.

Another observation is that I've never gotten in trouble for lying. Because I'm that good. I have a knack for knowing what needs to be said and done.

And if a little is good, then a lot is better, right?

I used to think like that. Before my life went from zero to crap in a week.

# A GOOD LIE FURTHERS
# YOUR AGENDA

By midmorning Monday, I had Katie Knowles believing that I suffer from a terrible disease. One that modern medicine doesn't recognize, can't identify and is powerless to treat.

I told her that I have chronic, degenerative, relapsing-remitting inflammobetigoitis. Which doesn't exist. I culled symptoms of mono, plantar warts, shingles, borderline personality disorder and a bladder infection, as well as listing a bunch of side effects from some TV ads for drugs.

Even for me, this was a whopper.

But I had to come down with whatchamacallit so that I wouldn't have to team up with Katie for the working-with-a-partner project in social studies this semester.

Cannot. Deal. With. Katie.

She's some sort of mechanized humanoid, made up of spare computer parts, all the leafy green vegetables that no one ever eats and thesaurus pages. We're only in eighth grade, but everyone knows she's already picked out her first three college choices, her probable major and potential minor and the focus of her eventual graduate studies. To Katie, middle school is a waste of time, so she takes more classes than she needs to and does extra credit the way the rest of us drink water. She's probably got enough credits already to graduate from high school.

The Friday before, we'd been assigned to be each other's partner for our social studies independent study project: a ten-page paper and an oral presentation in which we would "illuminate some aspect of our government relevant to today's young citizen."

Thanks, Mr. Crosby, way to narrow the scope.

We wouldn't have class for the next week so that we could go to the library or the computer lab to work on our projects. This was going to teach us about independence and self-determination. Or something like that; I wasn't really listening.

I really dig Mr. Crosby; he's pretty laid-back except when he starts talking about what he calls "government pork," and then he gets all wild and upset. I must have irked him somehow to get assigned to Katie. My best friend, JonPaul, and our buddy Jay D., who are the biggest troublemakers this side of a prison riot, were project partners, and even the Bang Girls (I call them that because they're BFFs who have identical haircuts with the exact same fringe hitting their eyeballs in a weird way that makes my eyes water if I look at them too long) had been paired. Before I could ask Crosby what I'd done to set him off, he'd announced, "Once partners are assigned, there will be no switching."

I am not a guy who gives in easily, so I spent the weekend thinking of ways to convince Crosby to change his mind, and avoiding Katie, even though she'd been calling, emailing, IM-ing and texting. It was only third period on Monday morning and already she'd left a couple of notes at my locker and had tracked me in the hall between classes.

"Kevin."

I flinched. Katie has one of those bossy yet whiny voices that make you want to stab pencils in your eardrums to make the noise stop. I turned and broke out a killer smile. I can always tell when it's time to crank up the charisma.

"Hey, Katie, I meant to—" I started, but she cut me off before I could come up with plausible and inoffensive reasons why I'd ignored her all weekend.

"It doesn't really matter." She flipped open her notebook and handed me a sheaf of papers. "I utilized the time by getting started on the initial research. You can see that I brainstormed about a dozen ideas we could examine that I believe to be unique and ripe for exploration. Why don't you take the packet home, read everything over, and then let me know by this time tomorrow, if not sooner, what you've decided? I'm okay with any choice you make, and we should, after all, be democratic about how this partnership functions, because of, you know, the class subject and all."

"Uh . . . yeah, right. I see that you, wow, you typed up—what's an abstract, again?"

"A brief summary and succinct explanation, the theoretical ideal, if you will, behind the project topic." She tapped her foot impatiently, probably wondering why I hadn't been writing abstracts since nursery school.

"Sure, that was what I was going to guess. You did an . . . abstract thingie . . . for all twelve ideas?"

"Of course"—she pushed her glasses a little higher on her nose—"because that kind of organization and attention to detail will enable us to make the best possible choice among our options. Besides, I'm sure I can put the seemingly superfluous work to good use in the form of extra-credit projects later in the year."

"Uh-huh."

"Like I said, why don't you take this home and—"

I cut her off. "No, I don't need to do that; let's pick number, um, seven. Yeah, that looks like a great idea."

"The analysis of data collected during the most recent national census about the underserved population and how they interact with and regard the government services structure, especially pertaining to the link between educational grants and future acts of public service?"

I really should have read her summaries, but it was too late. The analysis of the something census and how the something interacts with something as it pertains to something it was.

She beamed when I nodded, and I knew that I'd

somehow chosen right even though I didn't know what the peewadden she was talking about, and I was sure, if I'd tried, *really hard* and *for a very long time,* I could not have come up with a more butt-numbing topic.

JonPaul and Jay D. came over, grinning.

"We got a beauteous subject, Kev; Crosby laughed at first, but then he signed off on it."

"What are you doing?"

"Exploring the possibility of a link between the World Series and voter turnout in presidential elections," Jay D. said proudly.

"You know, like, if an AL team wins, does that mean more Democrats will show up at the polls, or," JonPaul explained, "will Republican voting habits change if the NL team wins?"

"That's not about the government, you moron. And it doesn't even make sense."

"It has to do with the executive branch; we're golden," JonPaul said.

"You're just jealous because we're going to spend a week cutting and pasting World Series highlights into a PowerPoint presentation," Jay D. said, smirking. "What're *you* doing?"

I studied the floor and mumbled, "The analysis of how something about the census something interacts with the something and pertains to something."

They snorted, punched my arm and left me with Katie, who had been rereading her notes and probably hadn't even noticed JonPaul and Jay D.

"You don't look so good, Kevin."

"I . . ." I would rather die than work with you on this monkey butt of a project, is what I wanted to say. But I heard myself saying, "Look, Katie, it's probably not fair that you got stuck with me, because I have . . . some medical issues that might prevent me from, er, living up to my part of the project. It's just too soon to tell—we're waiting on test results and some studies in Germany that have to be concluded."

"Really?" She looked intrigued, which was new, because Katie usually walks around with this distracted expression on her face, like she's busy figuring the square root of the prime number closest to the gross national product. "I'm fascinated by medical mysteries."

"Well, that's what this is, all right. No one can figure out what's going on. We've been to an endocrinologist, a cardiologist, a neurologist, an osteopath, a Reiki practitioner, an energy healer, a physical therapist and a physiatrist, because they"—I paused meaningfully—"specialize in chronic pain management."

She gasped. I'd had no idea until that very moment what a great audience Katie Knowles was.

Note to self: Katie is smarter than a NASA computer, but wuh-hay too trusting for her own good. Excellent.

I was feeling pretty lucky right then that JonPaul is a total hypochondriac who's always worried that he's coming down with something rare and dangerous. I could rattle off the names of all those different kinds of doctors like I was a fourth-year medical student because we spend a lot of time entering his alleged physical ailments in medical website search engines.

Katie leaned forward, and I whispered the many problems I'd been suffering, which had led to the diagnosis of chronic, degenerative, relapsing-remitting inflammobetigoitis. "It started with night sweats, which caused the dehydration. Then I developed mood swings, hair loss and cotton mouth. And, of course, there's the sensitivity to light, rapid heartbeat, dizziness, dry skin, loss of appetite and frequent thirst, which were worrisome. But all that wasn't nearly as bad as the muscle aches, migraines, gastric reflux, bleeding gums and mild to moderate confusion when fatigued."

I figured all this was icky enough to make Katie want to keep her distance but not so bad that she'd wonder why I wasn't in the hospital. Or quarantined.

She looked horrified. "Oh, you poor brave thing."

I nodded sadly and tried to look brave. Brave and wan.

"I'd, well, you know, I'd wondered about you. That maybe something was amiss," Katie said sympathetically.

Oh, you had, had you? But before I could blow my cover by sputtering something defensive, Katie saved me. Boy, did she save me.

"Look: I can handle the project for both of us."

I opened my mouth to pretend to talk her out of her selfless offer, but she raised her hand to shush me. "You were lucky to get paired up with me, because I don't know anyone else in class able to cope with this much responsibility on their own."

I could tell that Katie was actually relieved that she wouldn't have to work with anyone else, and I silently congratulated myself on my gift of saying the right thing to the right person. Without knowing it, I must have sensed that she'd rather work alone. Even if it was because her partner was chronically ill and that meant she'd have to share credit.

I'm a very intuitive guy.

"Are you even strong enough to be in school?" She peered anxiously over her glasses.

"Uh-huh. My medical team says that keeping things as normal as possible—while avoiding stress—is the best treatment."

"That makes sense." After looking behind her, she dropped her voice to a whisper. "Does anyone else know about your condition?"

"No. I haven't felt . . . comfortable enough to share this. But there's something about you; you're a really good listener, and a person feels like he can confide in you."

She squeezed my hand, clearly believing that my random symptoms weren't contagious. "Don't worry; I won't say a word. You just concentrate on getting better. I'll do the legwork and you can help with the revisions and fact-checking, okay?"

"That sounds amazing, Katie, thanks."

With a conspiratorial wink, she headed off to her next class.

Suh-weet! I'd essentially be proofreading—checking for errors and making suggestions about work that had already been done on behalf of "our team."

Look, I just wanted to get assigned to a different partner. Is it my fault that Katie volunteered to do the whole dang project? I think not.

Once again, my lie had created a win-win situation—I didn't have to work with Katie, and Katie didn't have to work with anyone.

And what was wrong with that?

# A GOOD LIE CAN SUPPORT
# ANY PLAN

The only people I don't lie to are girls, but that's because I almost never talk to them and it's hard to lie when your lips aren't moving.

Katie doesn't count. Not. A. Real. Girl.

My older brother, Daniel, says I'll outgrow thinking that girls are complicated and really emotional. My guess is that he's lying to me. But I never thought much about it one way or the other.

Until I was walking down the hall just after my talk with Katie, on my way to my locker, happy about how things had turned out.

Then I turned the corner in the upstairs hall on my way to lunch and fell in love.

Just. Like. That.

Tina Zabinski was standing by the drinking fountain with some of her friends, laughing. I heard her laugh and my heart gave this crazy lurch, and my breathing did a stop-start thing, and I got sweaty, and did other stuff we learned about in Family Life, stuff that marks the moment a male's physical maturation begins. I'd never been so glad to be carrying a math book.

I'd heard about love at first sight, but it sure had never happened to me before. In fact, I wasn't even certain you could count what was happening right then as love at first sight, because I'd known Tina since preschool and I'd probably seen her every school day for eight or nine years. But I'd clearly never really looked at her before. Or else she'd turned into the prettiest girl in the world since I'd seen her the past Friday.

I ducked inside the Spanish lab to study her through the window in the door.

I started to count the many colors of her hair— butter, honey, wheat, gold—and as I was racking my brain for ways to say *blond*, I realized that I had what it took to be the world's greatest boyfriend. I'd never cared about stuff like this before. But I cared then. In fact, I was starting to care so much I was having a hard time standing, because my knees felt weak and rubbery.

She must have felt me staring at her, because she turned and saw me peeking through the window in the door.

I waved casually like I hadn't just been caught gawking and started to walk toward her to see what it was going to take to get her to be my girlfriend— I am a very goal-oriented guy.

Halfway across the hall, I tripped. No, that's not right; I actually fell over my own feet, which felt like they were being remote-controlled by a spider monkey during a sleep-deprivation experiment.

"Hey, Kev, you okay?" Tina asked as she watched me peel myself off the seventh grader I'd trampled.

Had her voice always been so . . . soft? How could I not have noticed that? I must have talked to her a million times.

"Gunh."

That started out as "Sure, fine," in my head.

I blinked in surprise. For the first time ever, I couldn't speak. I'm never at a loss for words, so this was a new sensation.

I swallowed and tried again.

"Ereewah." My voice cracked. Oh, great! Puberty was hitting *now*. Here. In front of Tina. Good timing.

She looked at me curiously. I started to sweat. I felt drops, then streams, of perspiration slide down my ribs. I didn't dare look down—I was sure there was a puddle developing around my shoes. I stood very still so that I didn't accidentally splash Tina or send stink waves in her direction.

I tried taking a deep breath to get control of myself, but all that happened was a loud gulp, like in a cartoon when the bear eats the picnic basket whole.

Tina studied me. Probably wondering why she'd never realized I was socially retarded and had epic glandular problems. She didn't edge away nervously, though, or look around for an excuse to leave me standing there making weird noises to myself. Instead, she smiled.

Tina smiled at me.

Before I could tell her how much she had come to mean to me in the past three minutes and that I hoped she'd feel the same way about me—maybe not in the next three minutes, but soon—my arm was nearly yanked out of its socket as JonPaul jerked me down the hall toward the cafeteria. I waved nonchalantly at Tina with my free hand and hoped she wouldn't notice the sweat stains spreading down my shirt.

"Dude, gotta haul it if you don't wanna get the crusty leftovers." JonPaul bobbed and weaved through the crowded hall, unaware that he had ruined my great moment with Tina. I stared over my shoulder at Tina's right hip, which was all I could see through the crowd.

"You can let go of my arm now," I finally said after he'd dragged me around a corner. Oh, sure, *now* I can talk, I thought.

He grunted and dropped my arm, but he picked up the pace. JonPaul is very serious about eating on time.

"Hey, JonPaul. You ever been in love?" I tried to sound matter-of-fact even though JonPaul and I don't talk about feelings.

"No," he said. "Girls are germy."

JonPaul is a germaphobe. The mere thought of girls makes him whip out his hand sanitizer. JonPaul plays football, basketball and baseball and is roughly the size of a half-ton Chevy pickup, but he's a total wuss about his health. When he was done disinfecting his hands, he pulled a bottle out of his backpack and swallowed a couple of vitamins. Just to be on the safe side.

"Kev"—he jumped out of the way of some girl who might have been about to sneeze—"remember how we talked about how my cardio program will keep me from getting sick?"

JonPaul's workout was the last thing I wanted to talk about, when I had so much I needed to ask him about Tina. But because I am such a good friend, I *mm-hmm*ed encouragingly.

"It's all a waste of time unless I focus on nutritional balance and . . ." JonPaul kept talking, but I stopped listening. He obviously wasn't going to be any help at all on the Tina front, and she was all I cared about right then.

I nodded and *uh-huh*ed through lunch and, although I'm sure we sat with our crew like we do every day—Jay D. and Jay M., Scott Kahney, Greggie Hoffman, Todd Neiderloh, Kurt Sneed, the new kid I don't really know yet and Sean Sexton—my mind was on Tina. I couldn't taste a thing, I didn't hear a word. I just sat there, watching Tina eat a salad.

She was all I could think about all day. I spent every class writing down things I knew about her (she's got an older brother, she's on the swim team and she broke her arm in second grade) and questions I wanted to ask her (what's her favorite food, why does she feel Americans have taken so long to embrace soccer and does the idea of paranormal activity creep her out). It's a good thing I make such detailed outlines for my research papers, because I knew how to organize my thoughts and start making sense of what I was feeling.

By the time the final bell rang, I was newly aware that Tina sat directly in front of me in language arts, two people over and one behind in science lab, and kitty-corner in the cafeteria. I saw her after fifth period on the sixth step from the bottom in the south stairwell, and after eighth period, when I lurked outside her French class and followed her to the bus line, even though I walk home and don't take the bus myself.

I didn't dare try to speak to her again all day, and I wouldn't until I was sure that real words would come out of my mouth and that they were the best possible words to make her want to go out with me. I'd never had a girlfriend before and I'd never stammered and sweated like that, either, but I wasn't going to let any of that stop me. Millions of guys had girlfriends; there was no reason I wouldn't be able to figure it out too.

After school, I paced around my room, trying to come up with the best method to get Tina to notice me—in a good way—when I happened to glance out the window. I saw my four-year-old next-door neighbor, Markie, who I babysit for every week, playing war with his family's cat. I don't think the cat knew she was playing war, though: I think she thought she was asleep in the sun. Markie was on his belly, commando-crawling up behind her, ready to pounce when he got close enough. Good soldier, I thought, taking advantage of the element of surprise.

An idea started to form in my head, and I walked over to the shelf of books of military history next to my desk. All that reading was about to come in handy.

I'll read anything about war; I'm fascinated by the strategies and thinking of great military leaders. My mother always says, "I worry that I'm raising a future warmonger." But I knew she'd be proud of the way I was going to put all that research to good use.

Okay. Time to think. I sat down, tipped my chair back and started to thumb through the index of one of the books.

Obviously, the best approach to landing Tina as my girlfriend would be to study the way generals plan military maneuvers. I would utilize foresight, bravery, skill, careful timing, reconnaissance missions and the support of staunch allies to show her that I was the best possible boyfriend for her.

"What are the primary components of a good military campaign?" I asked my reflection, because I'd read about a general who talked to himself in the mirror to get psyched for battle.

"Go with what you know, use what you have, play to your strengths," I answered.

This was going to be a cinch. All I'd have to do was make sure Tina knew how amazing I was—without being conceited. Piece of cake, because I'm funny (I've always cracked myself up) and smart (I've never made a big deal about my 3.769 GPA) and popular (I wasn't sure she particularly liked my friends, but I had a ton of good buddies and figured that had to be a strong recommendation to a girl).

What girl wouldn't want to date a guy like that?

It's not that I thought highly of myself, it's that I really am a great guy. I'd never thought about it before, but once I looked at the evidence, it was obvious.

And if by some small chance all of that didn't work, I'd fall back on what I do best—I would lie.

That is, in military terminology, I would employ subterfuge.

But this was, I felt certain, the one situation where lies wouldn't be necessary. The truth was plenty good enough: I had what it took to be her boyfriend. I just knew it.

I didn't mind saying it (mostly because there was no one else in my room who would): "I'm a freaking genius sometimes. I really am."

# 3

## A GOOD LIE BEGINS WITH
## AN ELEMENT OF THE TRUTH

I was still lying on my bed, thinking that even her name was gorgeous—Katrina Marina Zabinski—and sounded like music (kah-TREE-nah mah-REE-nah zah-BIN-skee), when I heard a car pull into the driveway. My sister, Sarah, was dropping our brother, Daniel, off after hockey practice. I jumped up to run downstairs and ask her to take me to the mall with her, since I was going to need new clothes to impress Tina.

My mom was working late, like she always is; my dad was on one of his business trips, like he always is; and even Auntie Buzz, who lives in the apartment above our garage, wasn't home yet, and I'd been counting on Sarah for a lift.

But before I could take a step, the car zoomed back down the driveway.

I'm fourteen. Daniel's fifteen. Sarah's sixteen. We were born exactly thirteen months apart from each other.

Daniel had his learner's permit, which burned me, but Sarah had her driver's license, which killed Daniel. We also had Auntie Buzz's old car, which ticked us all off. We spent a lot of time on the driveway screaming at each other.

That wasn't the plan. The plan was that Auntie Buzz would go green by not having a car and we would save the Earth by carpooling. She'd showed us the scooter she'd bought and told us about the power walking she'd do to and from work and asked me to help her read the bus schedule. What wound up happening, though, was that Auntie Buzz, who owned a decorating business, drove her work van (which got terrible gas mileage, so where the green part came in, I'll never know) and we became the new owners of a rusted-out piece of junk that caused more problems than it solved.

When Auntie Buzz gave us the car, she'd handed us each a key. She wanted to be fair, though she didn't seem to care about being legal, since she was giving two unlicensed kids keys to a car they couldn't drive. Then she said, "Now, remember, you have to share."

Sarah's definition of *share* was that she drove our/her car everywhere she wanted, whenever she wanted, and made us beg for rides. "I'm the only legal driver," she kept pointing out, "and besides, you and Daniel never chip in for gas."

Daniel's and my definition of *share* was that, because we were part owners, she should have driven us everywhere we wanted to go, every time we wanted to go anywhere. Daniel jingled his keys at her and said, "We represent a two-thirds majority," while I reminded her, "Possession is nine-tenths of the law."

To be honest, I don't know what Auntie Buzz was thinking, giving three teenagers a car in the first place, but she only sees the positives of a situation, none of the negatives.

Things went from bad to worse at the beginning of the school year because my brother and sister were both in high school and I was stuck in that yawning chasm of nothingness, middle school. "And our school starts twenty minutes earlier than yours," they said, "which means you can't ride to school with us."

The "so there" was implied.

After our parents refused to intervene—"Your car, your solution," they said—I asked Auntie Buzz to mediate. I wasn't happy with her decision.

"You live close enough to easily walk to school, and high school kids have so many more activities, and it's just so nice to see the two older kids finally spending time together." She must have felt very King Solomon–esque, or, come to think of it, the very opposite of King Solomon, since everyone got something when he laid down the law.

So Sarah and Daniel drove to school together every morning, making a fast-food drive-thru breakfast run along the way. I walked and ate granola bars.

And then this: Sarah leaving with the car like I didn't even exist, as if there might not be someplace I needed to go in the afternoon.

Daniel and Sarah had ignored me once too often.

I had to make them see my point of view. Talking it out hadn't helped, screaming it out hadn't worked; it was time to take action.

I sat thinking about them for a little while. About their weaknesses. And how I might pit one against the other to my advantage with a few teeny, tiny little lies.

I smiled finally and then went to the kitchen for my favorite snack: a banana dipped in melted chocolate chips. Because creativity, my art teacher always says, must be nourished. Okeydokey.

Daniel came into the kitchen after his shower, grunted hello at me and grabbed a soda and a bag of sour-cream-and-onion chips.

"Where's Sarah?" I asked as I peeled my second banana. I concentrated on looking innocent, which is harder than you'd think, and I wished I'd practiced that in the mirror too.

"She said something about shoe shopping." He crunched and slurped his answer.

"That's weird"—I paused to lick my finger—"because she was whining all last week about being flat broke. Girls, go figure."

Daniel just kept wolfing down chips. I could tell he was going to need a nudge to see things clearly. Or, at least, from my point of view.

I shook my head. "She seems to have a lot of new clothes all of a sudden. Where does she get all that money, anyway? I hope"—I forced a completely fake laugh that anyone older than five days would have recognized as phony—"she hasn't been stealing."

He did a complete and perfect double take. Then he looked at me with huge, shocked eyes. Daniel's primary character flaw is that he's gullible.

"Nah. I don't . . . stealing?" He was thinking hard, and I hoped he was calculating the cost of Sarah's wardrobe and the price of gas.

Sarah works like a beast of burden: She's got a part-time job at the hospital; she babysits a couple of times a week; she occasionally works for Auntie Buzz; and she charges her friends to do their hair and makeup for weekend parties and dates. Our sister is a mogul-in-training and only complains about being broke because she loves to sound dramatic and put-upon.

But Daniel isn't aware of these facts. He doesn't particularly notice things, not if they aren't in a hockey rink or a computer game; he's not stupid, he's just not observant.

But I am. I'm a very observant guy.

Daniel was still thinking. "I heard Mom and Dad talking with Sarah the other day in the kitchen. They seemed really upset. I couldn't hear much, but I wonder if they were trying to figure out what to do about her stealing."

I pretended to look surprised. Then thoughtful. Then sad. I said, slowly, reluctantly, "I read an article in the newspaper the other day about the rise in teen shoplifting statistics."

Daniel looked at me disbelievingly. Then an expression of disgust crossed his face.

"Knowing Sarah, she probably made herself seem misunderstood so that they'd feel bad for her and let her off easy."

"She can talk her way out of anything." I shook my head in dismay. "I can't believe, though, that Mom and Dad didn't at least take the car away."

Bingo.

Daniel has always thought Sarah is spoiled and selfish and never gets what she's got coming to her.

"She's in all this trouble and she still busts my chops about giving me a ride to and from hockey practice? She's got nerve."

Just then Sarah came into the kitchen and, as luck would have it, she was carrying four or five shopping bags and looking smug. Her natural expression.

"You always get everything exactly the way you

want it, don't you?" Daniel snapped before he stormed out of the room.

"What's with Dannyboy?" Sarah asked me.

"He was all peevish that you always take the car because of your, what did he say? Oh yeah, selfish nature." I didn't bother mentioning that I had manipulated the situation and that he now thought she was a klepto. Oops. My bad.

"Well, if that's the way he feels about me, then—" Sarah has never backed down from a fight, and I knew exactly how the next five minutes were going to play out.

She went flying down the hall and started pounding on Daniel's door. His stereo volume increased to drown her out.

Just as Sarah started shouting curse bombs to get his attention, my mother came home.

She opened the kitchen door and looked at me. "Why do they sound like tiny demons from hell?" Without waiting for my reply, she marched to Daniel's bedroom and flung open the door.

"Sarah, give me your car keys. Daniel, yours, too. I've had it with this constant fighting. Now neither of you will be driving that car for a week and maybe I'll get some peace and quiet around here."

"That means I'll have to get a ride to school with Alex the greasy loser from across the street and his skanky girlfriend," Sarah moaned.

"Indeed." Mom was not impressed.

"And"—Daniel's voice was glum—"I'll have to bum a lift to hockey practice in Derek's deathmobile that reeks of jockstraps."

"That's what you get for not honoring the spirit of Buzz's gift by working things out with each other," Mom said.

A better person than me would have felt bad that Daniel thought Sarah had issues that led her to thievery.

And a more upstanding young man than me would have felt terrible that Sarah felt compelled to yell at Daniel:

"You're nothing but fecal matter and I wouldn't spit on you if you were on fire!"

"But I'm your brother." Daniel sounded genuinely wounded.

"You," she announced, "are a turd in the punch bowl of life."

Nice one, Sarah! Even Mom, who was back in the kitchen and sorting through mail, lifted an eyebrow in approval.

Two doors slammed. Silence.

"Ah, that's better," Mom said. "And how was your day, Kev? And have I mentioned that lately you're my favorite, and not incidentally quietest, child?"

Before I could answer, Sarah, seething, reappeared in the kitchen.

"I'm telling Dad."

"Be my guest," Mom snapped as she swept out of the room. Under her breath, I heard her say, "The next time he stops in for a visit." Her bedroom door shut. Then she opened the door and slammed it.

Blink.

Huh.

That was new. Mom is usually as cool as a cucumber and, as family fights go, this one was only about a 4 on a scale of 10; I've seen Mom reach out and catch sandwiches we kids have hurled at each other without losing her page in the book she was reading.

Mom had been working overtime because the bookstore she manages is short-staffed. Meanwhile, Dad's new promotion meant that he was always on a business trip. They'd both been crabby lately. I hadn't really noticed that until Mom slammed her door.

Sarah, having lost everyone's attention, slunk back to her room. I sat at the kitchen table and thought.

It occurred to me that our family didn't pay much attention to each other when we were together, which, once I thought about it, wasn't much to begin with. We were all so busy. And when we *were* home, everyone usually had his or her nose stuck in one of the books or advance readers' copies that Mom brought home from work.

My father always says she only works to feed our family's book addiction and that we'd be further ahead financially if she collected aluminum cans from the side of the freeway to recycle.

In the past couple of weeks, I'd been seeing Daniel reading some business book about how to unleash your inner hound to get ahead in sports; I'd read *Lady Chatterley's Lover* (because I thought it was dirty, but I couldn't find the sex parts); and, over supper, Sarah had been flipping through a baseball book about the steroid scandal. As for Mom, she reads so much and so fast that I can't keep up with her.

We read a lot, and we have great vocabularies as a result, but we don't talk very much.

Which kind of leads to a bad place, I guess.

I tried to shrug off a dark feeling I was getting

and recapture the warm sense of justice: Sarah and Daniel, carless too. I'm a guy who's all about justice. In a week they'd get their keys back, but they'd have a better sense of my point of view, and maybe they'd remember to give me a ride now and then.

I headed to my bedroom to start homework and tried to ignore the shiver that ran down my back when I passed three closed doors.

# A GOOD LIE CAN BE USED
# MORE THAN ONCE

**M**eanwhile, back to Operation Tina.

I was sitting on the front steps of school Tuesday morning before the homeroom bell rang, trying to finish an assignment while keeping an eye on Tina, three steps down, when it hit me: Classes were getting in my way.

It's not that I don't like school—I do. But wasting my time in class was a problem if I was going to make Tina understand what a great guy I was.

Out of the eight periods a day, I only saw Tina in three—language arts first period, lunch fifth period and science seventh period. Thanks to the social studies get out of jail free card, I could go to the commons and watch her during her free period while waiting for the perfect moment to dazzle her with my personality.

But I needed more free time. Classes were slowing me down.

A lesser mind would have accepted defeat, since the odds were stacked against me, but the best military leaders always find ways to eliminate obstacles. It was clear that I was going to have to bail on my Tina-free classes: Spanish, math, and gym and art, which alternated days.

I looked around the front steps and sidewalk, assessing my options. I saw Freddy Dooher, who's on the wrestling team. Normally I hate him because he's as mean as a snake during the season when he's starving to death, trying to make weigh-in before the meets. But that day I loved him because he gave me a great idea.

I dashed inside as soon as the first bell rang and ran to the Spanish lab to tell Señora Lucia that I'd recently begun student-managing the wrestling team. She's only at school two or three times a week because we share her with the other two middle schools in the district, so I didn't think she'd have a clue about the sports schedules. I didn't, and I'm here five days a week, all day.

*"Buenos dias, Señora."*

*"¿Cómo está, Señor Kev?"*

*"Bueno.* For a while now I've been wondering how I can add more to the school spirit. I've decided to become an athletic supporter." I snorted at my own lame joke. I wasn't sure the humor translated, because she kept organizing her stack of bilingual flashcards.

"So I'm helping the wrestling team, keeping track of scores and . . . like that."

*"¡Que peligroso!"* she said, clearly mistaking wrestling for extreme sheepherding or something riskier than a bunch of guys rolling around on stinky mats in the gym.

"Would it be okay if I missed some classes so that I can . . . help the guys get ready for . . . tournaments? I'll get the homework and reading assignments from Roberto."

*"¡Bueno!"* She beamed. She gave me a hall pass so that I could go to the gym when I was supposed to be in Spanish.

I hustled to get to homeroom on time. Once I was there, Brooke Daniels and her sickening boyfriend, Timmy Kurtz, caught my eye. They're Mr. and Mrs. Drama Department and really annoying—always eee-NUN-cee-ate-ing. It's really gross the way

40

Timmy lets loose with flying gobs of spit. He gives JonPaul total germ fits when he talks.

However, seeing them gave me another idea. Art! I asked for a pass from my homeroom teacher and blasted down to the art studio, where Mrs. Steck was counting tubes of paint.

"Mrs. Steck!" It's the only way to talk to her about anything, because she herself speaks with lots of exclamation points in her voice. "I'm working on the crew for the musical!" I blurted. "Can I miss a few days of class to paint scrims?!" I was glad I'd seen a rerun of *High School Musical* recently; I had my drama department terminology nailed.

"Kev! That's wonderful!" Mrs. Steck looked at me with admiration. "I always give extra credit to my students who paint flats and build sets!"

I hope she'll feel the same way about pretend walls on imaginary stages, I thought as I tucked her hall pass into my pocket.

Two down, two more to go.

On my way to language arts, I passed the school newspaper office, which gave me a new idea. Coach Gifford was about to discover that the athletic department was finally going to enjoy the editorial support it had long been denied.

I caught him as he headed into the locker room.

"Hey, Coach, gotta second? I'm gonna be writing for the sports section of the newspaper."

"Good work. I'm always available to offer a quote. Do you want one now?"

"Not just yet, thanks. But I was hoping it would be cool with you if I missed gym for a few days while I learned the ropes."

"Anything for some friendly press, sport." We fist bumped, he scribbled a hall pass and I turned to leave. "Don't forget to run a few laps," he bellowed down the hall after me. "Wouldn't want you to get flabby and out of shape."

I flashed him a thumbs-up.

Check. Check. And check. One more.

I thought for a few minutes, stymied about how to get out of math. Then the voice came from on high, the loudspeaker in the hall.

"Would all members of the student government please report to the auditorium at the start of the fourth class period? Thank you."

No, thank *you*.

Tina is the student rep for room 81. I knew this because I'd looked up her name on the school website the night before in my information-gathering process.

I'd skip fourth-period math and send Mr. Meyers an email alerting him to the fact that I'd taken over as the room 82 alternate. He'd be impressed by that, because he'd run for town council once and was always talking about "what a pleasure and a privilege it is for one citizen to serve another."

Even though all the information about the wrestling team and the musical crew and the newspaper staff and the student government could be verified on the school website, I'd never been a troublemaker, so no one would suspect I was lying and check up on me. I knew they'd want to think I was a good kid working his tail off to make the school a better place.

My friends would keep me up on homework and warn me about tests. I made a note: (1) Ask them to shoot me info about assignments every day after school, (2) text Katie that I'd been feeling feverish and achy, to keep her sympathies alive.

I'm really doing nothing more than increasing the value of my education, I told myself. Making mostly As had been getting too easy. Skipping classes would be a challenge if I wanted to keep my grades up. And

I did. But I had to make time to get to know Tina better. And, more important, to have Tina get to know me better.

She was worth anything it took to show her that I was the only possible guy in the entire school she should think about spending time with.

# 5

## A GOOD LIE HAS AN OUTCOME
## ADVANTAGEOUS TO ALL PARTIES

ike any good military mind, I decided that a direct assault was the wrong move. Too bold; better to start on the periphery and work my way in toward my final objective, gathering intel, studying the secondary targets in order to acquire data about the main objective. So I'd learn all I could about Tina's BFFs, find a way to make nice with them, crack their inner circle and then, *ding ding ding*, Tina would notice me and talk to me and, one thing leading to another, before you know it, I'd be her official boyfriend.

Tina's best friend, Connie Shaw, was also in the student government. Perfect. It was like the planets and the stars were aligning to ensure my success. Everything was falling into place, I thought as I strolled into my first-ever student government meeting and looked for my soon-to-be-girlfriend's best friend.

Connie is a troll. I'm not being mean; she just is. She's kind of . . . husky, I guess you'd call it if you were looking for a nice way to say that she's got a great future ahead of her as a load-bearing wall. And she's got a monobrow going too. I never would have noticed if Sarah hadn't practiced eyebrow waxing on me last summer.

"Won't hurt a bit, Kev, I'll pull it off clean and fast," she said before she ripped off so many layers of my forehead along with my eyebrow hair, you could almost see brain matter. I peed and screamed—a little and not so little, respectively. But now I notice girls' eyebrows.

Anyway, I walked into the student government meeting just as the president was calling it to order. JonPaul, of all people, was standing at the door, handing out copies of the agenda. I wanted to kick myself for not remembering that he was the other room 81 delegate. I have *got* to stop tuning him out all the time; apparently, he doesn't just talk about sports and illnesses. He looked surprised to see me, but we didn't have time to say anything because everyone was rushing to get seats. I wished he was in on my scheme so we could signal each other surreptitiously and look suspicious and in the know, like a couple of spies being used by the military to collect important data.

Instead, he headed up to sit on the stage with the officers and handed the leftover agendas to the person he sat next to. The lights were bright and it took my eyes a few seconds to adjust, but it was Tina! She was up onstage. All that prettiness and blond hair and soft voice and she's civic-minded, too. How could I have missed how perfect she was all these years? And what was the fastest way to get her to feel the same about me?

I scanned the rows of chairs and then hurried over to where Connie was sitting.

"Hey, mind if I sit with you? You can kind of show me the ropes and tell me what I missed."

Connie looked up at me. It was one of those stares girls can do—the kind where nothing is said but a point is being made. I don't speak wordless glance so I'm not sure what she was saying, but I sensed it wasn't good for me.

"I've never seen you at a student government meeting before," Connie said. Coldly, I felt.

"It's the social studies project," I explained. "I'm all of a sudden interested in the functions of government."

"Really?" Connie raised her monobrow at me suspiciously.

"Yeah, sure, I love government. In fact"—I frantically tried to recall that morning's announcements— "I'm worried, uh, concerned, really, one could even say dismayed, about the . . . referendum . . . thingie," I finished, and hoped I'd turn into a socially aware and deeply concerned kind of guy in the next 3.4 nanoseconds.

Connie furrowed her monobrow in shared worry, or concern, or dismay. It was hard to read one eyebrow.

"Yes"—I kept babbling, trying to win her over— "the referendum about the distribution of property tax income and how it's used to fund public schools and if the idea of a tax hike should be put on the upcoming ballot."

I had no idea how I remembered that.

Connie thawed a bit. "I'm glad you care about such an important issue. Sit down and I'll explain what's going on until you catch up."

I tapped into my ability to go on mental auto-pilot. My face looked interested and I made "um-hum" noises at the proper times. All the while, I was watching Tina and getting more annoyed with Jon-Paul, who whispered to her the entire meeting. I was sure it was just about his body mass index or the tensile strength of his ligaments, but still, he had her ear and he wasn't using it to talk me up.

The fact that he didn't even know he should didn't cross my mind.

By the end of the meeting, Connie had pushed her phone number and email address on me and I think I'd offered to serve on her committee to present ideas to the school board. She was going to argue the . . . distribution of something, and the something public ballot.

I wondered if she and Katie Knowles were close friends. If they weren't, they should be, because although I was looking at Connie, I was seeing a Katie clone. I'd have to find a way to tell Katie about Connie's committee and the presentation and, presto, she'd probably volunteer to help me out with that, too.

Then, when Tina and I were finally dating, I'd make sure Connie and Katie had the chance to hang out together and get to be BFFs. Minds like theirs, working together, could rule the world. And I was finding that they were very handy to have around. Plus, I was already starting to feel a twinge of guilt for the way I was about to take a lot of Tina's free time away from Connie.

Until then, though, Connie would give me insight into Tina's likes and dislikes so I could shape myself into perfect boyfriend material. And hanging around with Connie, I'd be hanging around with Tina by extension. And proximity would give me opportunities to catch her attention by being wonderful.

I don't know how dumb guys get girlfriends, I really don't. It's a lot of effort, and it seems to me that without my work ethic, you'd be screwed.

# A GOOD LIE HAS HUMOR AND STYLE

JonPaul came home with me after school to hang out and watch movies. But not until he'd asked if anyone else would be around.

"No, just us. Why?"

"Your mom and Sarah are okay and your Auntie Buzz moves so fast I don't think germs have a chance to land on her, but Daniel . . . well, he doesn't seem like a lather-rinse-repeat kind of guy, and I've seen how hockey players bleed on each other. That can't be sanitary."

"What about my dad? Does he give you the germ willies too?"

"No. Not since I got him to buy those preflight vitamin packs to ward off airplane-cabin viruses."

Bought them, gagged on them, flushed them, I remembered. But I didn't tell JonPaul; he'd have been so disappointed in my dad and probably too worried to come over to my house again.

Don't get me wrong, I love the guy, we've been friends since nursery school and always will be, but it's hard to get his attention. Once you do drag his mind off bacteria and injuries, he's okay. But keeping a conversation alive with him is a lot of work, and I worry that there aren't very many people like me who would put that kind of energy into getting past JonPaul's paranoid outer layer and finding the decent guy inside. It's not like our other friends bust him for the way he is, but I can tell they're not as understanding as I am.

JonPaul is nearly six feet tall, with shoulders as broad as a four-lane highway, and he can bench-press me. He's an über-jock and a gym rat, but he lives in such fear of illness that he never wants to get close enough to anyone to catch anything they might have or be carrying. I didn't understand how he could play all those full-contact sports if being touched and being breathed on were so abhorrent to him, but when I asked, he got a determined look in his eye and said, "I don't think about it during the game. I get in the zone and stay there. It's about discipline."

He washes his own equipment and uniforms after every practice and game, though, and he takes showers that seem like the kind that workers get after there's a chemical leak at a nuclear power plant. I heard his mother tell my mother that she has to buy industrial-sized bottles of bleach and boxes of detergent in bulk at the buying club.

I thought we were going to kick back, shoot the bull and watch a movie, but JonPaul couldn't relax until he'd disinfected his gym clothes. He tossed me a duffel bag.

"Hey, there's only one pair of shorts and a single T-shirt in here," I pointed out. "Are you sure you want to wash them all by themselves? We usually wait until there's a full load."

He didn't answer. I looked up to see him reading the ingredients on my mother's box of presoak powder. I was kind of surprised when he didn't ooh and aah.

Right. Time to change the subject to what

I wanted to talk about. I started the washer and we walked out of the laundry room and crashed on the couch in front of the TV.

"So, hey, you seemed to be pretty friendly with Tina Zabinski at the student government meeting," I said. "I didn't know you knew her that well. What's up?"

"Oh yeah, what were *you* doing there?" As I suspected, JonPaul had completely forgotten my surprise appearance that morning.

"Broadening my horizons. So, back to Tina— are you two friends?"

"No, not really. She's just, you know, around." He pulled a small lunch cooler out of his backpack and became completely engrossed in pouring out individual portions of raw almonds and golden raisins into cereal bowls he'd wrapped in plastic. Undoubtedly after sterilizing them.

I am not easily distracted. "What do you think about her?" I persisted.

"Oh, she's . . . hey, I only have enough organic peanut butter left for one sandwich. Wanna share?"

"No, I'm good." I peered into the jar of what looked like baby diarrhea and then jerked away.

"Looks like baby diarrhea, doesn't it?" He spread

it happily on some whole-wheat, flax-enriched bread and took a hefty bite. "This stuff is so good for your digestive system. Healthy turds float, bro, did you know that? The ones that sink are bad news and mean you're eating all the wrong stuff and poisoning your own body with toxins like preservatives and additives."

We. Are. Not. Talking. About. This.

I couldn't take it anymore, and as he started jotting down the details of his snack in his food log like some obsessive hippie survivalist scientist hybrid, I jumped up from the couch, hollering, "JonPaul, are you okay? Can you hear me? Don't go toward the light, come back to my voice!"

"What are you talking about? I'm just sitting here adding up my carbs and my protein grams." JonPaul looked totally freaked out. He should have—I'm very dramatic; I was totally committed to the moment, and I was selling this bit.

"You ate that peanut butter sandwich and twitched and your eyes rolled back in your head and, although it was only for a few seconds and I'm not one hundred percent sure, I coulda sworn you stopped breathing."

"Probably sudden-onset peanut allergies; I read about that on the AskADoc.com site the other day."

I could see that his hands were shaking. "Do I look okay?"

"Kinda." I studied his face, frowning.

"What's that supposed to mean?"

"You look . . . splotchy. And you seem a little . . . unsteady."

"I *am* dizzy."

"Low blood sugar," I said, nodding. "That's probably all it is. You should lie down for a while."

"Or maybe eat something?"

"And run the risk of choking to death on your own vomit? What if it's something more serious?"

"Yeah, buddy, you're right. I'm gonna bail, head home and go lie down for a while."

"Smart." I nodded some more.

JonPaul went off, limping slightly. He'd probably be checking his pulse and taking his temperature all night. That kind of behavior made me more certain than ever that, once he was pushed to batcrap-crazy extremes, he'd be forced to see the depth of his obsessions, and then he'd start to develop a more realistic perspective on the whole health nut thing.

I'd started out on the right foot.

I slid the movie into the machine and watched

the car turn into monsters by myself. I kind of missed JonPaul, but at least I could eat bananas dipped in melted chocolate chips and not have to listen to what the processed sugar and hydrogenated fat were going to do to my bathroom habits.

Connie called and talked at me about her committee idea for a while. She asked if we could get together on Wednesday or Thursday to do something and talk about the other thing. I wasn't really listening. I wondered if England had paid attention to everything France had to say during World War II. I didn't think so—they were allies, not buddies. That was how I'd think about Connie, too. She just didn't know we were on the same side, fighting for the good guys to win.

Then Katie emailed me an update of her project outline, with the topic sentences from every paragraph. She asked me to proofread her introduction; it was fine, really top-quality work. That was what I emailed back, even though I didn't read it. That's what Delete buttons are for.

The next day at lunch I could see the dark circles under JonPaul's eyes. He hadn't been in school all morning.

"I went to see the allergist. Got the scratch test," he reported. "I'm not allergic to *anything*."

"Great! But you can't be too careful, bud."

"That's what I said! But Dr. Culligan said I had to 'react adversely to the stimuli' before she could prescribe me anything."

"What's in your hand, then?"

"Markie's EpiPen."

"You stole an EpiPen from Markie? What if Markie has an allergy attack and needs it? I'm calling his mom to make sure he's got a backup."

"He's got a valid prescription and can get more anytime he wants. Lucky booger. Plus, there are about a million of them lying around over there—they'll never miss one. And I didn't steal it—he gave it to me."

"You just gonna carry it around waiting to stab yourself in the leg?"

"Yeah. Like you said—can't be too careful. I can tell that my glands are swollen. I think my throat is closing up. Am I wheezing? I think I'm wheezing. I definitely feel like I'm wheezing. Maybe I need an inhaler, too?" He held a carton of cold milk up to his nonfevered head.

Friends don't let friends wuss out like this.

JonPaul's weakness could easily be exploited by unscrupulous opposing teams if it wasn't rooted out of him while he was still young. I was doing this for his own good. As well as the teams he played on.

Looking at it from that perspective, I was helping to make JonPaul a happier, better-adjusted person.

And then he could focus on suggestions about the Tina situation, and if she happened to find out that I was a very thoughtful guy and the best friend anyone could ever have, so much the better.

But I forgot to mention it to him. I was calling Markie's mom.

## GOOD LIES MAKE THE WORLD
## GO ROUND

"**B**uzz is one crazy broad." That's what Dad has always said about my aunt.

"Buzz rocks." That's what Sarah and Daniel and I think.

No one's sure what Mom thinks. But she must like having her sister around, or she wouldn't have offered to let her move in above our garage. My aunt has lived there as long as I can remember.

When I got home after school, I decided to see if Auntie Buzz had any advice on how to get Tina to realize how incredibly perfect I would be as a boyfriend. Because if anyone knows about relationships, it's Buzz. She's been married three and a half times.

The half comes from a spring-break marriage in Cancún when she was in college. "It probably wasn't even legal in the first place, so it only counts as a halfsie," she told me once.

Auntie Buzz is very high-energy. The double shot of espresso at the coffee shop across the street from her office is called the Buzz in her honor. Dad watched her knock back a few espressos once and muttered to me, "That kind of energy must have been hard on all those husbands."

Sarah and I work for Buzz on weekends and during school vacations, carrying boxes of swatches and tassels and paint chips and tile samples and carpet books from her office to her work van and back again. Decorating is a heavy business.

She hires Daniel and his hockey team to move furniture. They work dirt cheap and don't, Auntie Buzz says with a happy smile, belong to a union. Plus they work overtime for pizza and doughnuts and that's the kind of payment Auntie Buzz can afford. "I'm not good with money, and my projects always go over budget," she explained.

Auntie Buzz was sitting at our table when I walked into the kitchen, tapping away on her laptop. Mom had a late meeting, Dad was on Generic Business

Trip Number Infinity and Beyond, Daniel had practice and Sarah was working, so I had privacy to bring up the Tina thing with Buzz.

"Hi, Buzz."

"Hiya, Kev."

"Whatcha doin'?"

"Putting together a demo reel so that I can be hired as the host of a network television show. Or cable, I don't really care. Just so long as it's national and pays well. I'll do any kind of show."

"Uh, why?" Even though I was dying to ask her about Tina, a person doesn't just ignore this kind of information.

"When you work for and by yourself on commission and the government is sending you registered letters, you need to get creative about your income stream."

"I didn't know you were getting registered letters."

"It's a recent development."

"So . . . how much trouble are you in?"

She shrugged and then scowled in the direction of a canvas bag near her feet. It was filled with a ton of unopened envelopes. Some of them had green Registered Mail stickers on them and were from the Internal Revenue Service. I'm only fourteen, but those people scare me. Tax time each year at our house is not pretty—Mom and Dad drag out shoe boxes full of receipts and take over the kitchen table for days on end, and there's a lot of sighing and frowning and *clickety-click-click*ing of the calculator.

Adults, I've noticed, are usually terrible with money. I thought about the sock full of cash I have hidden in my pajama drawer. I'm an excellent saver.

"How much do you owe?"

"I'm not going to open the bills until I have the money to pay everything." She looked more jittery than normal.

"Do you want me to find out for you?"

"You're only fourteen years old—exposure to that kind of stress might kill you or make you sterile, and I don't want to be responsible for you not being able to have children someday."

"I don't think that's going to happen if I read a few—twenty-seven—letters." I hunched down and thumbed through the stack of envelopes.

"Can you put them in chronological order for me? I'll find an accountant to deal with everything first thing on Monday."

Monday is always Auntie Buzz's favorite time to handle a problem.

"Do you have any plans for, uh, solving your financial . . . situation other than getting your own television show?"

"Why should I? I'd be a natural on TV, and the network—or the cable companies—would be crazy not to hire me."

Buzz and I were more alike than I'd suspected; that was exactly the way I think. Self-confidence is everything for military geniuses, liars like me, and decorators in trouble with the government. All of a sudden, I felt warmly toward my aunt—a little parental, even.

When Sarah and Daniel and I run through our allowances and ask to borrow money from our folks, we get a huge lecture, and then they make it a teachable moment. No one ever gets punished in this house, because Mom says we should "experience the consequences" of our actions so that we can "benefit from the learning opportunity."

I thought Buzz could get a lot out of a teachable moment. And I was just the person to teach her. I was the answer to her prayers—she just didn't know it yet.

She was in a lot more trouble than Sarah or Daniel or I ever were, so she'd need more help and a bigger moment of teachabilityness, and if that isn't a word, it should be.

She didn't even notice when I took the bag to my room. I sat on the floor and separated the invoices from the checks. Then I went downstairs to the family computer in the basement and sorted through the boxes of software until I found the bookkeeping program Mom uses for her store. On the way back to my room, while Buzz was still on her laptop, I quietly rooted though her purse and grabbed her checkbook. I could have shaved her head for all she would have noticed. She was typing away, and her fingers must have been breaking land-speed records. I saw an empty coffeepot on the table next to her.

I took the disk to my room, installed the program on my laptop and whizzed through the tutorial, and in no time flat, I was entering debits and listing credits. I was so glad we'd done an accounting section in math a couple of weeks ago or none of this would have made any sense to me.

About an hour later, I'd balanced Buzz's checkbook and discovered that she had a ton of money. She just never recorded the deposits. By the time I'd set up a bill-paying system and gotten everything entered and paid, Auntie Buzz had turned a nice profit in the past quarter.

I felt a little drunk with success, so I read the letters from the tax folks. I didn't know what she was so freaked out about. The letters told her to call the 800 number and set up a payment schedule. I grabbed the phone and called the number and, deepening my voice a little, had a friendly conversation with a lady named Ms. Young who was completely understanding about Buzz's dilemma in these tough economic times and suggested a monthly repayment plan. I read the number of Auntie Buzz's checking account to Ms. Young, who said she would send Buzz the paperwork right away.

I could have told Auntie Buzz that her problems had been solved, but what kind of lesson would that have taught her?

I heard Auntie Buzz make a fresh pot of coffee and introduce herself for about the twelfth time to the webcam on her computer so that the network— or the cable companies—could see what a great personality she had on camera.

I had second thoughts about asking her for advice on Tina when I heard her pretend to banter with her imaginary cohost ("Well, Chuck, you *would* say that, hahaha"). One. Crazy. Broad.

I went downstairs to check my email. I sent a long note to Connie that I cut and pasted from the town council's monthly minutes, throwing in a lot of *heretofore*s and *therewith*s. Then I emailed Katie that I'd just gotten back from a lab draw and—good news!—my white blood cell count was down. I said yes to a request from Markie's parents to babysit the next day, and I IM'd JonPaul to see how he was feeling. My buddies had sent me homework from the classes I'd missed, so I started to tackle that pile of mindlessness.

Truth be told, as much as I liked looking at Tina and devoting all my time and energy during all my free hours to thinking about making her crazy about me, it was already Wednesday and I still hadn't come up with any brainstorms to get her to like me.

A few more pointless days like this and I was just going to lie to her. This truthfulness thing was a whole lot harder than my spur-of-the-moment inventions.

# 8

## A GOOD LIE TAKES ON
## A LIFE OF ITS OWN

I took a break from homework to check my phone for new texts later that evening and nearly jumped out of my skin.

"Mom!" I leapt up from the computer desk in the basement and raced upstairs to the kitchen to find her. I'd heard her come in, and had heard Buzz leave, a while ago. "JonPaul and his cousin, you know, the one in college they call Goober? Well, they have tickets for the Blind Rage concert festival at the Kane County Fairgrounds this weekend and they want to sell me one and take me with. The greatest part is that Buket o' Puke 'n Snot is headlining."

"Buket o' Puke 'n Snot? Can't say I'm familiar with their body of work."

"You've heard them, you just don't know it. 'I Could Kill and Eat You,' 'You Suck, but Let's Hook Up Anyway,' 'Anarchy Rules,' 'Dissension Is the Answer,' 'Loving You Is a Pit of Death.'"

She shuddered and shook her head. "Poetic though they sound, and I appreciate that you've just described both tender ballads of love and socially prescient commentary, I still don't believe this rings any bells."

"Dude and the Jailbaits are playing too, and Skullkraker."

"Delightful bill. How much is this . . . ode to dark despair going to run you?"

"Tickets are two fifty."

*"Two hundred and fifty? Dollars?"*

"I have money from working for Auntie Buzz, and I'll pay."

"Yeah, you will."

"The thing is, we gotta camp out the night before because it's open seating so we need to get there early to get good spots near the stage. And it's a two-day festival with a whole bunch of up-and-coming bands in addition to the headliners, so we'll leave on Friday and then come home Sunday, late, when it's all wrapped up. Better make that early Monday morning."

"Kevin. Son. Are you crazy? You think your father and I are going to sign off on allowing you, a fourteen-year-old boy, to go off with some . . . Goober creature for two days and nights of antisocial music—and I use that term lightly and with apologies to musicians and composers everywhere—without parental or even coherent adult supervision?"

"What's your point?"

"No. *N. O.* That's my point."

"Can we discuss this?"

"We just did." She gave me that look. The one that said I was about to go somewhere I didn't want to go. And that I was bound to make things worse for myself if I pressed the issue. I know my mom; she's got no wiggle room. Yes/no, right/wrong, black/white, good/bad. End of discussion.

I stormed back to the family room downstairs, pounding hard on each of the ten steps to let her know that Kevin. Was. Not. At. All. Happy. About. What. Just. Happened.

Because I wasn't speaking to her, I didn't say anything as I turned right around and stomped back up the stairs to the kitchen to make myself a banana with melted chocolate chips, and then, just for good measure, I accidentally/deliberately burned a bag of microwave popcorn so that the whole house reeked.

She went to the living room with a book.

I pondered our discussion as I ate my snack. It's times like this when loopholes become a guy's best friend. What had she said, again? Something about my father? Hm. Doesn't seem to me that he was consulted at all.

I'll fix that.

I sent Dad a quick text, stressing the wonder of the situation and the once-in-a-lifetime aspect of the offer. My dad's a big music fan, so I knew he'd be predisposed to thinking it was a good idea. I forgot to mention I'd already spoken to Mom. Forget, neglect, tomato, tomahto.

The great thing about my dad being gone all the time is that he always responds to text messages and emails from us at the speed of light.

"snds gd. ill txt mom. hom soon."

Fab. I get to go to the concert *and* Dad breaks the

news to Mom. I hoped she'd be so mad that he went ahead and okayed the concert that she wouldn't even notice I'd gone behind her back to get permission.

I took the phone to my room to call JonPaul and tell him and Goober to count me in. Mom must have heard from Dad, because I heard her cell beep with an incoming text message. She remained in the living room, though. And didn't say a word. The hairs on the back of my neck rose.

Playing one parent against the other has always been strictly forbidden in this house. But it wasn't my fault Dad was never home to know what was going on.

I told myself my actions were justified because Mom would have let Sarah go in a heartbeat—she's "trustworthy," which, of course, just means my sister's smart enough to never let our folks find out what she's done or where she's been.

And Mom would have felt okay about Daniel going, because he never does anything without his hockey team and they're all so terrified of messing up and getting benched for the next tourney that they never get in any trouble. Bunch of brownnosers. Bloodied brownnosers with missing teeth.

I was tired of getting the short end of the stick in

this family just because I was the youngest. The ends justified the means.

I could see myself strolling into school after the concert and walking past Tina wearing my Buket o' Puke 'n Snot T-shirt. That would be the icebreaker I needed to talk to Tina and make her aware that I was a cool guy into alternative music who went on weekend concert trips with college students.

I was trying to find my black jeans and figure out which shirts I'd pack. Dig out the old sleeping bag, too. I wondered how much spending money I'd have to bring.

I heard the front door slam and my father's voice call out, "Helllllllllooooooo . . ." I stopped moving and I held my breath.

Dad was home.

I peeked out my door and down the hall. I had a perfect view of the kitchen.

Mom must have heard Dad. And learned how to telekinetically transport herself, because she was immediately standing in front of him in the kitchen.

She wasn't wearing a happy face.

"Hi, honey," Dad said absentmindedly as he shuffled through the pile of mail on the counter, and therefore did not notice her clenched jaw. Or fists.

"What a trip. I'm beat. Oh, and that new dry cleaner you took my suits to last time is a moron."

"Michael, you treat this house and family like a hotel and staff members. You never do the laundry or handle the dry cleaning yourself, you haven't gone grocery shopping or cooked in years and you have never once cleaned the cat box. And then you undermine my authority by giving Kevin permission to go to a concert I'd already said no to."

"We have a cat?"

"Yes! His name is Teddy."

"When did this happen? Last week when I was in Philly?"

"Three and a half months ago when you were . . . gone. Like you always are."

Is he *always* gone? I wondered. Yeah, I guess he is. I mean, he's traveled a lot for work for as long as I can remember, but once I heard that Dad didn't even know we had a cat, I realized that he'd been gone nearly all the time lately and that, even for this family, he hadn't been paying very much attention to us when he *was* around. He was always frowning at his PDA or reading reports or . . .

Wait. Just. A. Minute. Here.

Come to think of it, I hadn't been paying much attention to Dad or what he'd been doing lately either.

JonPaul once dared me to bite down on a wad of tinfoil. Being an idiot, I did. The same shock and pain and nausea zinged through me now when I realized how . . . detached Dad had become.

We've always taken it for granted that Dad goes on tons of business trips; Sarah scoops the little soaps and shampoos and shoeshine cloths out of his shaving kit, and Daniel has more pens and badge holders than any fifteen-year-old kid on the planet. That's really all I think of when Dad crosses my mind these days—the junky stuff he brings home for us and the work he's always preoccupied with between flights.

I couldn't remember the last time Dad and I had hung out and watched a ballgame on television together or when all five of us had sat down at the dinner table or . . . well, anything much more than hellos in the hallway and notes to each other on the fridge about schedules and—in Daniel's and Sarah's cases . . . and Mom's and mine . . . and now Mom and Dad's—fighting with each other in the kitchen.

Everyone was so busy—work, school, part-time

jobs and friends—and I guessed . . . I guessed we'd just gotten used to doing without Dad.

Man. You miss a little in this house, you miss a lot.

I was still staring at the floor, trying to make sense of what was going on in the kitchen, when I heard my mother blow her nose. She didn't have a cold. She didn't suffer from allergies. She must have been crying. This was really bad.

My dad started talking, but I couldn't hear anymore; I was frozen in place in the doorway of my bedroom, clutching a pair of jeans.

I looked and saw Sarah standing at the bathroom door, her flatiron for her hair in her hand, and her mouth wide open. She too had heard everything—the bit about our cat, and Mom crying. Daniel was in his doorway, his head cocked, listening.

Sarah unplugged the iron and jerked her head at me as she passed me in the hallway. She snapped her fingers at Daniel.

We moved, unnoticed, past the kitchen, where my parents were standing in the middle of the floor silently looking at each other. Sarah led us out of the house and down to the curb, where she'd parked our/her car.

We all climbed into the car with jerky, unnatural movements like we'd recently been cut out of full-body casts and hadn't yet become reacquainted with our full range of motion. Sarah sat back in the driver's seat and took a deep breath, staring out the window at Mrs. Ebeling unloading groceries from her car two driveways over. Daniel sat next to Sarah in the front, looking down and picking a blister off his thumb like it was the most important thing that was going to happen all day. I sat stiff and tense in the backseat as if I was being graded on posture.

"Well," Sarah finally said. "That was . . . ugly."

I grunted, and Daniel made a sound that I couldn't decipher.

"In Dad's defense," Daniel finally piped up, "Teddy's not the friendliest cat who ever lived. I can see how Dad wouldn't have noticed him, because Teddy's always hiding. Most of the time you can only see his tail, and that's if you know where to look. Or," he added slowly, "if you look at all."

"That's the thing, Daniel: Dad *doesn't* look." Sarah was still studying Mrs. Ebeling as if the secrets of the universe, or at least of our family, could be found by determining the most effective manner of bringing groceries into the house. "And besides, the cat is not the problem; Dad not knowing he exists is merely a symptom of what's wrong with this family."

"How long have you known things suck?" We all asked each other the same question at the same time. If it hadn't been so sad, I'd have been impressed.

"A few months," Sarah admitted. "I asked them about it last week, but they said everything was fine, that they just had normal family issues to work through."

"When he went away for over a week for the third time in a month." Daniel was still working on that blister.

"About twelve minutes ago," I said. "But I also realized, about eleven minutes, fifty-five seconds ago, that I am beyond dense."

Sarah and Daniel nodded.

"What do we do now?" I asked.

Sarah glanced at me in the rearview mirror. "Oh, god, Kevin, you look horrible. Put your head between your legs and take deep, slow breaths. And don't barf in my car."

*"Our car!"* Daniel and I roared together at her.

She looked startled. Then mad. Then she started to laugh. Pretty soon she was laughing so hard I couldn't tell if she was laughing or crying.

Then I realized she was laughing *and* crying.

Daniel and I were too.

I didn't understand what had just happened. Everything had been going so well. I mean, I guess not, but . . .

## A GOOD LIE SHOWS YOU
## THE TRUTH

The next day, I just didn't feel like myself. Sure, I watched Tina during class and at lunch and in the hall and on the way to the bus, and she was still so pretty that she made my heart twist.

I met with Connie and we discussed whatever it was she was talking about; it's easy to be a good listener and make people think you're part of the conversation if you just say "What did you do then?" a lot, because that way they think you're paying attention, impressed with them. I think I said yes to something she had planned for next Monday at six-thirty in the evening, but I'm not sure what it was.

I even let Katie corner me in the hallway after

school and go over her outline again because she'd changed seven words since the last time she'd shown it to me and she wanted to make sure I approved. And I agreed with her that apathy was going to ruin this society. Or something.

JonPaul and I walked home together. He'd been wearing a motion-sickness band around his wrist because, he said, he was queasy all the time. He had a portable, disposable heating pad wrapped around his midsection because he thought his lower back was going into spasms. He lifted a pants leg so I could see the Ace bandage he'd wrapped around the ankle he swore was strained. And he carried a packet of wet wipes to scrub down his desk chairs and locker handle. He showed me a face mask in his backpack. "I'm just glad it's not cold and flu season," he whispered, "or I'd have to wear it. I'm just carrying it for security."

It was only Thursday and I'd only been ditching class for four days, but I was getting homesick for my regular routine.

I'd somehow staggered through a long and weird day, but when I saw Auntie Buzz through the kitchen window as I got home, I headed straight over to Markie's house for my babysitting gig without even dropping my stuff off in my room first. I wasn't up for watching Buzz's demo reel or hearing about the friendly-faced Buddha she needed for the Tibetan prayer room she was designing.

The now EpiPen-free Markie is a sheer terror.

I never feel right about trying to get out of babysitting, though, because his parents always seem so worried I'll say no and sound so grateful when I say yes. I usually dread it, but the day after the Kitchen Scene, I was glad. And I hoped his folks would stay out really late. Because I didn't want to run the risk of seeing my folks. For the first time, Markie looked good by comparison.

His parents call him precocious; I looked it up, and it does not mean the personification of an ear-splitting, nerve-jangling, head-pounding, exasperating plague that makes you long for deportation from your own country.

Little kids smell funny—like blue cheese and day-old socks and dog butt. Markie smells like all that, plus he's so freaking hyper and chatty that I know why his parents make such a fuss about "date night" just to get away from him once a week.

Sarah thinks they go out to romantic dinners and take ballroom dance lessons or see black-and-white foreign movies with subtitles and deep meanings. I'm pretty sure they park their car in the empty lot behind the bank and just sit there enjoying the silence. As well as checking off the boxes on their countdown to when Markie turns eighteen and leaves home.

The only good thing about spending the afternoon and evening with Markie was that I wouldn't have to think about what was going on with my folks.

On top of having a weird smell and the attention span of a fruit fly, that day Markie rushed me at the front door with a buttload of disgusting questions. Like he does every single time I come over. He must save them up for me.

"Dutchdeefuddy, where do farts come from? What are boogers made of? Have you ever tasted pus?"

Oh yeah, and he has this habit of beginning every sentence with the word *dutchdeefuddy*. Which does not mean anything. In any language I can find on the Internet. I finally decided that it must be like *shalom* or *aloha* and has as many meanings as necessary.

I always have to fight the urge to put Markie in a cardboard box in back of the furnace in the basement, securely closed with duct tape. Tied with stout rope. And swaddled with some sort of soundproofing material.

But that kind of babysitting doesn't get a guy paid. So I sighed and answered his questions. Like I always do.

"Farts are made of methane produced during the digestion of food in the small and large intestines. Boogers are the thickened or dried mucus that the cells in the nasal cavity need to function. And don't taste pus. Ever. It's a terrible idea. Kind of like the time I told you not to shove baby carrots up your nose and then eat them."

Then, grossed out by my efforts to educate a young mind, I sent him outside to play with the kids next door. When I looked out the window a few minutes later, Markie had seemingly cloned himself and there were fifty, sixty, I don't know, *hundreds* of him running around the yard. I shook my head to clear my vision and made a careful head count.

Three. Three small children plus Markie. They were just moving so blazing fast that they looked like a crowd. Sounded like one too. I bet Hell sounds a lot like a bunch of little kids shrieking.

The only solution was storytime. Little kids are suckers for stuff like that. And it quiets them down like a tranquilizer gun.

I rounded them up, dumped some dry cereal in a bowl—because you can always get on top of the situation with little kids by offering treats—and put my creative powers to work.

"Well," I began, "once upon a time, there was this guy. He was a . . . pirate-magician-dragonslayer-quarterback-sailer-musher-trapper who owned a carnival. He lived in suburban hedges waiting to find tiny soldiers for his army of puppy-sitters, who don't have bedtime and can eat pizza for breakfast with potato chips and chocolate milk. He recognized them by the balloons they tied to their clothes."

I was just getting into the story and wondering how it was going to play out, because I'm such a good storyteller that I'd fascinated myself, when the four kids jumped up, squealing for balloons. I blew up balloons until my cheeks ached and I was light-headed from oxygen deprivation. I tied the balloons to the kids' arms and sent them outside. Thing 1, Thing 2 and Thing 3, along with Markie, sat quietly under the lilac bush, and I congratulated myself. Mary Poppins, eat your heart out.

Then I read the World section of the newspaper to see if there were any international military developments I needed to catch up with that would inspire

me in my plan to make Tina think I would be a ter-
rific boyfriend.

Eventually, though, Markie's friends got called
home for supper and I was looking down at one
grubby kid with a limp balloon trailing behind him.

"Dutchdeefuddy, play with me."

"Why don't you watch a video?"

"Bo-wing."

"How about getting out some of your toys?"

"Bo-wing."

"All of them?"

"Uh-huh."

"Well, you could—"

"Dutchdeefuddy?"

"Yeah?"

"What's a 'vorce?"

"A what?"

"Mommy's getting one. What is it?"

It was like looking at a tiny me.

What the sweet screaming monkeys was in the
water in this neighborhood?

"Is it bad?" Markie asked.

I sighed and wondered what to say and if anything was going to go right for me that day.

"Well, Markie, it's not good."

His little face looked so miserable I wanted to kick myself. See? This is why I lie. When I lie, everyone always looks happy.

I thought of all the things I could tell him: 'Vorce is just another way to say his dad's a superhero—the very one I'd told the story about earlier—going off to save puppies and kittens; his parents will probably patch things up; or 'vorces aren't that bad, everyone's having them, don't be a baby and let it get to you.

I squatted down and looked him in the eye.

"A divorce means, well, that your mom and dad aren't going to be married anymore. But . . . you'll still be a family. Just different."

"Daddy's leaving again, isn't he?" he asked.

"Yeah, probably."

"Oh."

Yeah, oh; that's about the only response there is to news like that. Smart kid.

Then Markie said something that completely blew me away.

"Dutchdeefuddy, I want to be just like you when I grow up."

"Why?"

"'Cause when I asked everyone else about the 'vorce, they didn't tell me the truth. But you did."

"And that's a good thing?"

"Uh-huh, 'cause now I know."

Well, sure, every kid should have a full working knowledge of 'vorces, I thought.

Then Markie said the second most astonishing thing ever.

"You're my dutchdeefuddy."

"What does that mean, anyway?"

"Best, most favorite buddy. In the world forever." He slipped his little paw into my hand and looked up at me with the sweetest smile I have ever seen in the world forever.

All those times, I'd thought he was babbling, and here the kid had been telling me how much he liked me.

"Thanks, Markie, you're my dutchdeefuddy too."

Maybe the truth, in small, preschool-sized doses, wouldn't be such a bad thing after all.

Markie, holding my hand and swinging his feet as he sat on a kitchen chair, looked pretty calm.

The opposite of how I felt.

Maybe Dutchdeefuddy was on to something.

# 10

## A GOOD LIE CAN TURN ON YOU

I'd gotten home late from babysitting the night before. I hadn't told Dutchdeefuddy's parents about our talk. I was feeling about as wiped out as they looked. Romantic dates, right. My guess was that they'd been in a lawyer's office.

When I got home, I avoided my family. Or they avoided me. Every door in the house was closed, with someone behind it. Alone. Even the door to the basement was shut, which meant that either Mom or Dad had camped out downstairs rather than share their room with each other. And Buzz didn't swing by our kitchen on her way up to her apartment to say hi like she always does.

I didn't sleep well, thinking about Markie and his parents. About me and my parents. About me. About how I lie to everyone. All the time. About everything. The only totally truthful thing I'd said lately was when I'd told Markie his folks were splitting up. And that had seemed to go a lot better than anything else had.

It was Friday morning and I figured I'd pushed skipping classes about as far as I could, but since the week was mostly shot, I'd take this one last day. I'd make it an even week and start fresh on Monday.

I chewed a granola bar as I walked to school and thought it might not be a bad idea if I dropped back from a 10 to a 5 in the lie department. Before things started getting out of hand.

Not that I expected they would, of course—I still had everything under control.

I'd start by telling Katie the truth about my health and begin doing my part on the assignment. We had until next Friday; I could easily make it up to her. No sweat.

I caught her in the hall by the front doors before the bell rang as she headed toward homeroom.

"Hey, Katie, I gotta come clean with you: I'm not really sick. I was just trying to get out of doing the project," I blurted.

I couldn't read her face and I felt nervous because of the way she wasn't looking at me. So I started talking again to fill in the silence. Besides, the sound of my own voice always calms me down.

"But I feel really bad about it. I know there are only a few days left before we have to hand in our project and make our presentation. What should I get started on, boss?" Sucking up is always a good plan when your back's against the wall.

"Now? Nothing."

"What?"

That was *not* how this scene had played out in my head as I walked to school—she was supposed to be happy I'd confessed and secretly pleased that she could rely on me in the last few tense days of finishing up. Not to mention relieved that I wasn't sick. Then we'd share a good laugh over what a rascally sense of humor I had and would bond over the experience. She wasn't getting the big picture here. She was totally ruining my great plan.

"Everything's done—the research, the final draft, everything; all that's left to do is hand in the paper and make the report to the class." She still wouldn't look at me.

"Well, yeah, but there's got to be something I can

do. What about fact-checking? I could go over the PowerPoint and maybe jazz it up. Maybe I can handle the oral presentation? You know, take that burden off your shoulders? I'm great in front of an audience."

She shook her head. "I told you: everything is done. You can't put your name on the project if you didn't do any of it and you're not really sick. And I'll get in trouble for cheating if Crosby finds out about our deal. I'm going to hand in this project as mine alone."

"What about me?"

"You'll have to do your own."

"But it's due next Friday! Everyone else had an extra week and a partner."

"Then you'll have to make really good use of your time. And"—she did look at me here, and her glance made my blood run cold—"it's your own fault that you don't have enough time and a partner."

"I know you're probably mad at me—"

"You used me."

"No, that's not—well, yeah, I guess I did, but—"

"I should have known that disease was phony. I'm embarrassed that I was stupid enough to believe you."

"I'm very believable," I said, trying to comfort her. She didn't look comforted.

"It was kind of a joke." I tried to explain. "See, my best friend is always weirding out about health things and I kind of had improbable illnesses on my mind because it's all he ever talks about, so I—"

"Whatever."

"Katie, please . . . you can't be serious."

"You should be glad I'm not turning you in to Crosby. I'm doing you a favor, letting you dig yourself out of this mess."

She looked at me. Her eyes might have been a little sad, but her mouth was a tight, straight line.

"You're on your own."

Then she walked away from me.

Right past JonPaul.

Who had been waiting to walk to our lockers with me like he does every morning. He'd heard. Everything.

"What was that about?" He looked away from me as he carefully peeled the magnetic sticky patches that detoxified his cells off his wrists and slid them into a pocket. He unclipped the mini-sanitizer from the zipper of his backpack, too.

"It was a . . . misunderstanding."

"Katie doesn't seem like the kind of person who makes mistakes."

"Uh . . . yeah . . . well . . . see, the thing is—"

"Unless you say, 'The thing is I jerked everyone around this week because I'm selfish and stuck-up and I think I'm so much better than anyone else that I can make fun of them,' I don't want to hear it."

I couldn't speak.

What do you say when your best friend has lost his mojo because you tried to reduce him to a paranoid bundle of nerves terrified of going into anaphylactic shock? Even if it was for his own good.

"How do I make this right?"

"I don't know. I'm not Katie or Mr. Crosby. And I have no clue what you were doing at the student government meeting the other day. I don't know why you've skipped Spanish and art and gym and math all week. But I guess it has something to do with all these crazy stories I've been hearing all over school the past couple of days about you writing for the newspaper and joining the theater crew and becoming part of the wrestling squad and that you and Connie Shaw are going on community-access cable TV next week to debate the mayor. I thought it was another Kevin or maybe another four Kevins, but it's just the one. It's you, all right."

"I mean about you. How do I make things okay with you?"

JonPaul, without saying a word, turned away from me like I was something a fully suited hazmat team would avoid, and walked down the hall.

I remembered part of a coded message that the English used on the radio during World War II to alert the French Resistance to rise up against the German occupation: ". . . wound my heart with a monotonous languor."

I knew just what that felt like. The wounding part.

And I remembered, too, that the definition of surrender isn't to give up, but to go over to the winning side.

If they'd take me.

## A GOOD LIE REQUIRES
## A GREAT APOLOGY

FUBAR.

It's one of the all-time great military acronyms, and it stands for Fouled Up Beyond All Recognition.

I. Could. Relate.

But I wasn't going to panic just because things looked bad so bad so very very bad. Like the good general I knew I could be, I would take bold action, I would show no fear, I would stride, godlike, straight into the jaws of adversity. I wasn't exactly sure *what* I'd do yet, but I knew *how* I'd do it.

Katie had said so and JonPaul had proved her right—I was on my own. I'd gotten myself into this mess, and I had no one to turn to for help to get out of it.

So I went where I always go when I don't know what to do—I headed for the library to organize my thoughts and hammer out a battle plan.

I grabbed a computer station near the back and started making notes listing how I'd messed up. When I was finished, I sat back and reread my efforts.

Wow.

People who say today's generation has no work ethic would take that back if they saw how busy I'd been in one short week.

I'd be lying (and I'm *not going to do that anymore*) if I said that the thought of just waiting for everything to clear up naturally and hoping for the best hadn't crossed my mind. That would have been the path of least resistance. And it looked appealing.

But lying low would show a weak character, and that was not how I wanted everyone to think of me.

There was only one solution.

I was going to have to admit to everyone what I'd done, take responsibility for my actions, express regret for the pain I'd caused, accept the consequences of my behavior, make sure they knew I was serious about making it up to them and then never act like that again. The perfect apology.

The only downside was that a one-size-fits-all letter wasn't going to cut it. I was going to have to write specific letters to everyone.

I grabbed a thesaurus off the shelf, because there were only so many ways I knew to say "I'm sorry" without help.

Luckily, I've always been a very articulate and persuasive guy. I'd never needed either quality as much as I would now, though.

I apologized my miserable butt off. I confessed. Acknowledged. Asked for forgiveness. And promised to change my ways. I pretty much groveled.

I don't know why the popular phrase is *truth or consequences,* when it's really more like *lies and repercussions.*

While I was working on my letters, my cell started buzzing like crazy. We're not supposed to use cell phones in school, but I'd broken so many rules this week, what was one more?

I slipped my phone out of my pocket and snuck a peek at the screen. Auntie Buzz.

She sent seven rapid-fire texts, because Buzz

required 917 characters to make her point, with lots of ALL CAPS and tons of exclamation points!!!!!!!!

Buzz was in a communicative mood for someone who was SO MAD AT ME SHE COULDN'T SPEAK!!

The bank had called to ask her to sign some paperwork authorizing the direct-withdrawal program I'd set up with the tax lady. At first Auntie Buzz didn't know what they were talking about, but now she did and, "Mister, am I FURIOUS!! WHO do U think U R 2 MEDDLE w/ my financial affairs + VIOLATE my PRIVACY that way and does UR MOTHER kno she's raised such a SNEAKY person?!"

I texted Auntie Buzz a message that took fifteen screens because I needed 1,974 characters to explain what I'd done, that I was only trying to help and that I'd fixed everything for her. I apologized for the MENTAL AGONY (her words) that I'd put her through and expressed my remorse that she was BESIDE HERSELF.

I was three letters into my other apologies before Buzz got back to me.

"U R out of a part-time job 4EVER. And I don't want 2 C U 4 15 years. Or until Sunday dinner. But don't expect me 2 sit next 2 U or pass U the rolls. EVER!!! Maybe UR only fired 4 a week. I'll have 2 THINK about THAT!!!!"

I felt bad, but there was a little part of me that smiled, because I could tell she was getting a real kick out of this.

I hoped everyone else would find the same kind of satisfaction in yelling at me and then everything could eventually go back to normal. I was realistic enough to accept that everyone was going to be angry at me for a while, though, no matter how amazingly I apologized.

I sat there writing letters all morning, and I was exhausted by lunchtime. The simple truth is far from simple.

But I was starting to feel better than I had all week.

# 12

## A GOOD LIE DEMANDS
## SUBSTANTIAL AMENDS

After the longest morning of my life, I printed out all the letters I'd written, signed them and started delivering them face to face, like a man, like a soldier.

Katie took the letter from me in the hall as if she would have preferred I'd handed her a steaming pile of fresh horse manure. But she dropped it into her backpack, not the trash, and I took that as a positive sign. I could only hope she'd read it during her 12.5 minutes a day of downtime, even if she couldn't resist editing it before returning it to me for corrections and a clean second draft.

Mr. Crosby was at his desk. He looked surprised

to see me. He read my note, glanced up and said one word. One letter. "F."

I nodded and left. For the first time I could think of, more talking wouldn't help.

I have to admit that I was relieved that Señora Lucia, Mrs. Steck, Coach Gifford and Mr. Meyers weren't around when I went looking for them.

But at least I *tried* to find them. I didn't have time to search all over school; I had to keep plugging along on the Kevin Spencer Apology Tour. And although I wanted to be brave and manly and all those good soldierly things, I was happy to slip their notes into their mailboxes; I didn't particularly want to face another four failing grades on a Friday. Monday would be soon enough. Only a fool rushes bad news.

I had a plan B. Win back respect and trust. But now was not the time for it. Plan A, A-for-Apologies, this week. Plan B next week.

JonPaul took my letter when I found him near his locker, but as I turned to walk away, he said quietly, "I gave your concert ticket to Greggie."

I'd expected as much. But inside I screamed: *Nooooooooooo!*

I stood outside the girls' restroom and waited for Connie to come out. I handed her my note and said,

"As you read this, just remember that I am great at oral presentations." I walked away fast.

I'd heard once that the best apologies don't make a bad situation worse by further hurting the person you're apologizing to, so I hadn't admitted to Connie that I'd used her to try to get to know Tina; that would be cold. I wrote that I'd been trying to get out of classes and had maybe fudged a little on how genuinely excited I was about student government, but she could totally count on me for the debate, and the left is my good side on camera. Maybe a joke could lighten the mood.

It was difficult to write the apologies. But the hardest part was going to be waiting to see if they'd be accepted. A person can't hurry forgiveness.

The play director, the wrestling coach and the newspaper editor weren't even aware that I'd screwed them over, but I'd written to them anyway.

I found the drama teacher, whose name I didn't know, sitting in the lotus position in the middle of the stage. I set my backpack down in the wings, kicked off my shoes, padded over and sat on the floor next to her. It took me a few minutes to get both my feet on top of the opposite thighs, but I managed.

"I don't mean to interrupt when you're ...

meditating," I said quietly and, I hoped, peacefully so that I wouldn't ruin her calm mood, "but I want to volunteer to work on the musical."

She didn't answer or open her eyes, but she'd stopped humming, so I knew she was listening.

"I'm going to leave you this letter I wrote." I set it on one of her open palms as it rested on top of her knee. "I'll do whatever you need—manage props, work the lights, sweep the stage. My email address is in the letter. Uh, *namaste*."

Next I dashed to the assistant gym teacher's office. He's also the wrestling coach.

"Speak," Mini-Coach growled at me from his desk, where he was doing paperwork. He didn't even turn around.

"Yeah, uh, hi, you don't know me, but, uh, I'd like to be the student manager of the wrestling team."

"Uh-huh . . ."

"So I'm just gonna leave this letter I wrote here on the chair. You can get in touch with me when you're not so busy."

"Unh." He waved a hand.

"Good talk. You take care now." I backed out of his office. I don't know how JonPaul does all those sports if this is how coaches communicate.

When I got to the newspaper office, a staff meeting was in progress. I slid to the back of the room and pretended I belonged. Not very well, though.

"You." I looked up to see the editor pointing at me. "Who are you, what do you want, when did you decide to turn up, where did you come from, and why are you late?"

"I'd like to work for the newspaper. I'll write copy or deliver the papers to classes or clean the newsroom or change ink cartridges in the printers. I have some writing samples here for you." I handed him some of my research papers and short stories, which I'd printed out at the library.

By the end of the school day on Friday, I was pretty happy that I hadn't found the ideal moment to speak to Tina all week. One less person to apologize to. And at the rate I'd been going, I'd have messed things up with her and lost the chance to make her see that I was her perfect guy. When the air had cleared from my disaster, I'd focus on making her know all the wonderful things about me.

While trying to make sure she never heard a single thing about this week, that is.

# A GOOD LIE HURTS A LITTLE LESS
# WHEN IT'S OUT IN THE OPEN

I finally staggered home from a truly craptastic day. I wanted to crawl under my bed with my old stuffed bunny. Maybe take up thumb-sucking, too, because I was going to need some more coping skills. I knew I'd have to face my family sooner or later, but I was beat and hoped I'd have just one more night of closed doors and silence. I'd talk to them in the morning. I had a flash that Auntie Buzz had been showing some solid thinking when she came up with her "I'll deal with it first thing on Monday."

But Mom and Dad and Sarah and Daniel were waiting for me when I walked through the door. They were standing in the living room, trying to be casual, as if we habitually stand around together in the same room and it's nothing to be alarmed about.

Mom looked like she'd been crying and Dad looked like he might have barfed, but at least they were next to each other.

"Everything is going to be fine," Mom said right away, and I could tell that they'd been rehearsing because of how quickly and surely she spoke.

"This was a blessing in disguise," Dad continued, but from Mom's glance at him, I saw that he had gone off-script and was improvising. Mom jumped back in.

"We're going to start seeing a marriage counselor and probably try some family therapy, too. It's going to be a little weird for a while, but things will feel normal again pretty soon."

Dad took it from there. "I'm going to try to transfer to another division where I won't travel, and if that doesn't work out, I'll look for a job where I'm not gone all the time. But your mother and I believe that everything is going to be fine with us."

I felt a flicker of hope. That quickly died with Dad's next words.

"Now—Kevin. We got some calls from your school," he said. "We *really* need to talk about that.

Buzz called too. I couldn't understand a word because she was talking faster than normal and that's really saying something, but she's upset with you. And Daniel and Sarah have an interesting story about how they came to forfeit their car keys. And your mother and I need to remind you that you do not ask one parent permission when the other has already made the decision."

If life had a sound track—and sometimes I think that's a great idea—those *dunh dunh* gavel sounds from that legal show would have sounded then. And if I'd been starting a band right that very minute and needed to give it a true-to-life name, it would be All Hell Raining Down on Kevin. *Buket o' Puke 'n Snot* didn't do the situation justice.

"You certainly have been busy," Mom said. "I'll give you that."

"It's easier than you think to wreck a family," I said.

"You didn't wreck anything."

My eyes stung and my throat closed, tight and burning. I took a few minutes to stare at the floor until I was sure I could speak without squeaking or choking.

"I am so sorry for everything. I spent the whole

day at school writing apologies to everyone, and"—
I dropped my bulging backpack on the floor with
a thunk—"I've got all the work I need to make up
from this past week right here."

"I'm impressed by your initiative," Mom said, "but
that's not going to get you out of the punishment
your father and I have been talking about."

"You're going to have to earn the money for your
driver's ed class next year," Dad said. "We paid for
Daniel's and Sarah's, but the situation you caused
with the car this week . . ." He trailed off.

"I understand."

"No allowance for a month, you're grounded for
two weeks and we have a list of jobs around the house
and yard with your name on it."

"Okay."

"What were you thinking?" Mom asked, holding
her temples.

"I had this idea—well, it doesn't matter what
I thought, it was a boneheaded plan and everything
turned out horrible. I was trying to help Buzz, really;
you'll see, I made everything better. But I went about
it all wrong. I know that asking Dad about the concert was shady, but I never thought it would make you
two so mad at each other. And I couldn't think of any

other way to get Daniel and Sarah to see things from my point of view. They never listen to me and all we do is fight and it's two against one and the whole thing with the car has been a mess."

"Things between you three won't always be this intense," Mom said. "I have faith that you'll stop fighting as you get older."

"You'll appreciate each other more," Dad said. "The age difference will matter less and less."

Sarah and Daniel and I exchanged dubious glances.

"It's almost," Dad continued thoughtfully, "like you're triplets. Think of it: you'll be in college together, get married at around the same time, and maybe your kids will be close in age."

Mom snorted, but she was smiling at Dad as she spoke. "I'm pretty sure you only think like that because when you're on the road you watch those reality television shows about people who have weirdly large families."

Dad grinned back. "Maybe so."

Daniel scratched his head. "Wow. Kev. You . . ." He trailed off.

"Yeah."

He flopped onto the couch, tipping his head back

and closing his eyes. I knew just how he felt—exhausted to the bone. I glanced at the grandfather clock in the corner and was shocked to discover it was only four-thirty. I'd really packed a lot of revelation into one short day.

Mom and Sarah must have realized how weird we looked standing around in the living room, because they sat down on the love seat together. Dad dropped onto the couch next to my brother and threw his arm around Daniel before tipping his head back too. I shifted from one foot to the other, watching them.

"Kevin."

"Yes, Dad."

"Come sit next to me."

I had never been more grateful to sit next to my father.

He put his other arm around me.

I caught Daniel's eye on the other side of our father; he studied me for a long minute. His eyes were kind, though, and finally he smiled, looking remarkably like Markie.

Even Sarah winked at me from across the room. Of course, she flipped me the bird, too, but for Sarah, that was pretty warm and fuzzy. She leaned her head against Mom's shoulder and glanced at the book lying next to Mom on the love seat. "Oh! You're reading *To Kill a Mockingbird*. I love that book. Read it out loud. Like you did when we were little."

Mom smiled and opened the book. "'When he was nearly thirteen, my brother Jem . . .'"

Daniel and I sat with our father's arms around us for a very long time, listening to Mom read to us.

## A GOOD LIE IS AN OXYMORON

First rule of lies: Keep it simple.

Even though I know better, I forgot that bit for a while.

I also forgot what I learned in science class: For every action, there is an equal and opposite reaction.

For most of the weekend I sat at the kitchen table and did my homework. Every assignment was completed, every page was read, every paper was written and ready to be turned in.

I also did a cubic ton of extra-credit assignments that I came up with on my own to try to get back on all of my teachers' good sides—plan B. The paper I wrote for Crosby was about dishonesty in politics in the twenty-first century. I thought he'd appreciate the irony. I sure did.

I got to school super-early Monday morning and I ran all over, handing the stacks of work to Señora Lucia, Mrs. Steck, Mr. Crosby and Mr. Meyers. They didn't smile or nod or look approvingly at me in that heartwarming way teachers always do in made-for-TV movies when the troubled student has turned over a new leaf.

Clearly, they'd talked with each other about me, or else there's a playbook in the faculty lounge on how to handle students who ditch classes and lie, because each of them said the exact same thing.

"Unless you get straight As for the rest of the year, you're looking at summer school. And I'm giving you detention for three days."

That seemed fair.

Katie narrowed her eyes when she saw me in the hall, and radiated loathing.

Reasonable.

But maybe, I thought, she won't wind up swindled by a con man someday because of having known me. There's got to be a silver lining somewhere.

I was worried that I'd probably lost the best friend a guy ever had. But I knew I had to find JonPaul and give him the chance to tell me to drop dead and then never talk to him again. He deserved that much. I caught him at his locker.

"Are you going to keep sending me notes like we're fifth-grade girls?" He punched my arm and I knew we were good. Whew.

Then he reached into his backpack and handed me the Buket o' Puke 'n Snot T-shirt that he'd bought me at the concert.

Best. Friend. Ever.

Jay D. and Jay M., Scott, Greggie, Todd, Kurt and Sean, however, were a whole 'nother story. The guys went all Amish at lunch and shunned me. I walked up to the table where we always sit together and they looked right through me. They got over it, though, when they saw that JonPaul wasn't mad at me anymore. And the fact that I bought them all monster cookies from the cafeteria didn't hurt my cause.

Connie was a little cheesed off that I'd lied to her about being into government, but then I handed her a file folder.

"What's this?" she asked.

"An abstract of our argument for the debate tonight."

"A what?"

"A brief summary and succinct explanation, the theoretical ideal, if you will, behind our position." Katie would be so proud of me if she knew I'd paid attention to her.

"Really?"

"I read up on debating over the weekend. And I made an outline for us to follow and another of points to rebut our opponent's likely arguments. I put myself in his shoes and then worked backward to strengthen our position."

I walked away while her mouth was still hanging open. But she was nodding. Leaving on a great exit line is awesome.

The director of the school musical had set up a meeting to discuss the responsibilities of the house manager.

I'm kind of digging this theater thing. Plus, there's a cast-and-crew party on closing night.

The wrestling team and gym class situations aren't working out as slick for me as everything else. Coach Gifford and I chatted on the phone over the weekend. Turns out he'd gotten hold of my letter and signed me up as a probie wrestler. Not a student manager. My first practice is Tuesday, but he'll also see me after school for three weeks to run laps and do pull-ups and climb the rope because "it's good old-fashioned sweat and hard work that'll knock some sense into that head of yours. And I expect favorable articles about my teams in the newspaper."

I've always sensed that he has a mild mean streak, but, well, at least I'll get really buff. And JonPaul probably has lots of remedies for sore muscles and will tell me the fastest way to stop puking after I run. I'm looking at this experience as if it was basic training. Yikes.

Next, I'm writing a few sports articles for the newspaper. Considering my flair with words, how could I not be an awesome reporter? I'm going to start with an incredibly flattering interview of Coach Gifford.

Plus, Tina's on the swim team. The paper doesn't feature nearly enough profiles of student athletes. Meaning interviews with pictures.

Dutchdeefuddy's parents came over Sunday afternoon to tell me they're officially splitting up. But Markie's getting the house in the divorce settlement; he'll stay put and his parents will move in and out according to their allotted time with him. They're still going to want me to babysit every week because they think I'm such a good influence.

That's cool. Because every little kid (and probably even the not-so-little ones) needs a dutchdeefuddy he can count on.

Auntie Buzz wound up sitting next to me at Sunday dinner and passing me the rolls and acted like nothing ever happened with us.

A tiny part of me knew it was Buzz's way of saying thanks for all the checkbook magic I did.

She said she'd hired an accountant to manage things.

She didn't wind up applying for the TV gig after all. She was so hyped on espresso when she taped her audition that "I sounded like I was speaking chipmunk." But she didn't seem too disappointed, especially since her finances are okay now.

Mom and Dad and Sarah and Daniel and I have been speaking very quietly and walking very lightly; I'm sure bomb squads train this way.

And we're all going to have to get used to having Dad around all the time. Because of his seniority in the company, he was transferred to another department, and now he'll only have to travel a few times a year, and he's talking about taking Mom with him when he goes.

Mom finished reading *To Kill a Mockingbird* to us and hauled out James Michener's *The Source*. "It's a watershed book," she said. "You'll love it."

"It's a bazillion pages," we said. But everyone smiled when she licked her finger and said, "'Chapter One: The Tell . . .'"

Sarah and Daniel and I have agreed to drive to school together in the mornings. They'll leave a little later than they'd like and I'll get to school a little earlier than I want to, but we can cruise through the drive-in at Donut Deelite for long johns or at BurgerBurgerBurger for breakfast sandwiches. There's something really nice about scarfing greasy carbs with your brother and sister in the morning. Breakfast really is the most important meal of the day.

The whole family is going to start having dinner together every night, too. But Mom's not much of a cook, and I don't think anyone's ever going to get used to the slow cooker spewing out what Daniel refers to as gelatinous goo. You'd think a woman who works in a bookstore would have stumbled into the cookbook aisle by now, wouldn't you?

But we'll be together. And maybe Sarah and Daniel and I should learn to cook.

The truth really does set you free. Who knew?

Well, everyone, I guess, except me.

The only thing is—I still haven't gotten the chance to make Tina see that I could be the world's greatest boyfriend. But I'm working on that. . . .

**Gary Paulsen** is the distinguished author of many critically acclaimed books for young people, including three Newbery Honor Books: *The Winter Room, Hatchet,* and *Dogsong.* He won the Margaret A. Edwards Award given by the ALA for his lifetime achievement in young adult literature. Among his Random House books are *Masters of Disaster; Woods Runner; Lawn Boy; Lawn Boy Returns; Notes from the Dog; Mudshark; The Legend of Bass Reeves; The Amazing Life of Birds; The Time Hackers; Molly McGinty Has a Really Good Day; The Quilt* (a companion to *Alida's Song* and *The Cookcamp*); *How Angel Peterson Got His Name; Guts: The True Stories Behind* Hatchet *and the Brian Books; The Beet Fields; Soldier's Heart; Brian's Return, Brian's Winter,* and *Brian's Hunt* (companions to *Hatchet*); *Father Water, Mother Woods;* and five books about Francis Tucket's adventures in the Old West. Gary Paulsen has also published fiction and nonfiction for adults. His wife, Ruth Wright Paulsen, is an artist who has illustrated several of his books. He divides his time between his home in Alaska, his ranch in New Mexico, and his sailboat on the Pacific Ocean. You can visit him on the Web at GaryPaulsen.com.